The Autobiography

of

Wayne Helaire

Beauty Will Save the World . . .

WAYNE HELAIRE

authorHOUSE®

AuthorHouse™
1663 Liberty Drive
Bloomington, IN 47403
www.authorhouse.com
Phone: 1 (800) 839-8640

Published by AuthorHouse 11/12/2018

ISBN: 978-1-5462-5722-6 (sc)
ISBN: 978-1-5462-5720-2 (hc)
ISBN: 978-1-5462-5721-9 (e)

Library of Congress Control Number: 2018910302

For guardian angels watching over us my mother, my dad, my sister Elsie and my brother Glenn...

Beauty, bu'ti, n. [O.FR. biaute, FR, beaute,beauty, from LL bellitas, bellitatis,beauty, from L. bellus beautiful] An assemblage of perfections through which an object is rendered pleasing to thine eye; those qualities in the aggregate that give pleasure to the aesthetic sense; qualities that delight the eye, the ear, or the mind; loveliness; elegance; grace; a particular grace or ornament; that which is beautiful; a part which surpasses in beauty that which it is united; a beautiful person, especially, a beautiful woman.

From: THE NEW WEBSTER ENCYCLOPEDIC DICTIONARY OF THE ENGLISH LANGUAGE

Outline for the Conclusion of
The Fall of 72

My Heart
Goes
With You...

When I heard
the news
that you
had died,
I simply
sat
and cried
and cried
Lord, Lord
not Glenn,
of all the
news it
could have been,
It struck me
like a lightning
bolt
out of the
clear blue
sky
Lord oh Lord
why; why
did he
have to die..
I may as well
question
the morning dew,
Glenn,
my heart
goes
with you...

A Painting in My Mind

Images of mother
will never
fade away
I can see her
in the sky
each and every
sunny day
like a painting
in my mind
she melts
the snow away
with a voice
like a sunshine
forever
in my heart
she'll stay

I've got the cutest little Olympia typewriter. It is so cool I can not believe its mine it's sort of like a magic lantern it turned on my creative juices it gave me a reason d'etre to put down my thoughts and feelings about life in general what's it all about? My mother passed away on August 13 2002 unbelievable something of a mystical experience to be there in the room with her knowing that she could take her last breath at any moment, and when she did it was so surreal it's like a painting in my mind

Black and White
"My Mom, the Movie Star"

I've always wondered why I loved old black and white gangster
films especially the ones with Humphrey Bogart
and James Cagney (the roaring
twenties), sepia colored photographs and old
black and white photographs in
my mom's old photo albums every time I
would come home for a visit I would
go through each and every photo album my mom had, searching for old
photographs this one particular time in 1995 I discovered this torn and
tattered sepia colored wallet picture of mother. I was absolutely stunned
my mom was positively drop dead gorgeous it could have passed for a
publicity photo of some 1930's movie star. I
was so excited of course I had to
find out how old she was when this picture
was taken when I asked her she
said, "Wayne, I think I was 19 at the time this
picture was taken I said "mother,
you looked like a "movie star" this brought
a beautiful smile to my mom's
face. After having sears and roebuck restore
this photo (it cost $89), which
turned it into a masterpiece, I was convinced
that mother should have been a
movie star. I had an epiphany this explains
everything, my love for old black
and white films black and white photos, sepia toned pictures my love of
movies stems from the fact mother had the
look of a legendary movie star.
No hyperbole is too great for my mom..

Writing Journal
Of
Wayne

Working Title

Black and White
"My Mom, the Movie Star"

Notes and Ideas

An old photograph. A picture is worth a thousand words

Working draft

Character and plot notes

Memories of Mother

"Syrup and Biscuits"

Most of all I remember her smile, then the soft, sweet voice offering words of wisdom and encouragement how did you learn to make the biscuits? I would always ask everytime mother made her mouth watering melt in your mouth composition of Martha White self-rising flour and crisco shortening (it had to be crisco) her biscuits had to be made in heaven because nothing tasted better in the morning or anytime for that matter than her hot freshly made biscuits and Steen's pure cane ribbon syrup with a glass of cold milk and if we were to add bacon or ekrich beef smoked sausage and scrambled eggs to go along with the biscuits and syrup it was like nirvana or you could say it was the equivalent of the Davis/Helaire breakfast Valhalla I would always tease her about starting a restaurant or marketing her biscuit receipe she would always just laugh and smile that lovely smile of hers and say that I was prejudiced and that I was only saying it because she was my mother partly true but in reality everybody felt the same way mother was famous for her biscuits along with whatever else she cooked in essence she was a gourmet cook every meal she ever made was worthy of a 5 star restaurant her file gumbo was divine the only ingredients she used were chicken ekrich smoked sausage (beef) dried shrimp onions and garlic (cut up) and gumbo file first she made the roux with flour and the onions and garlic then she added the chicken to make a sort of chicken stew which was fantastic in itself I remember dad preferring the stew over the gumbo to me, they were equally stupendous her Sunday roast with potato salad rice and gravy cornbread (exquisite) candied yams mustard or collards greens her fried chicken with pinto beans rice and cornbread I could go on and on the combination of mothers angelic persona and gourmet cooking was like a 1-2 knockout punch once you experienced those two from her you were forever in love with her

Writing Journal
Of
Wayne

Working Title

Memories of Mother

Notes and Ideas

Mother's Notoriety in the Kitchen

Working draft

Syrup and Biscuits

Character and plot notes

The love of a mother for her children and grandchildren and how the love was returned to her.

"Beauty Will Save the World"

The Autobiography of Wayne Helaire

What does
it mean
to be alive?
Father
died
Then
mother passed,
I can't
take
it
anymore,
wondering
what other
tragedies
life has
in store.

Can I trust my instincts about love? Mother and Dad were so full of life and love. Always happy and smiling. Two loving parents and just generally good people.

Fall of 72

Where do I begin? All I know is that it's time for me to return to school after being in L.A. all summer. Had a marvelous time. L.A.'s weather can't be beat

It's hard to believe that I'm a sophomore in college.

My freshman year was very rewarding. Met a lot of nice and good people. Being in the freshman honor's class was the best thing that ever happened to me. Everybody became real close friends.

Well anyway I'm arriving in Baton Rouge and it's typical summertime weather in that it's hot and humid. The pollution here is extreme, air pollution that is The air is about fifty per-cent sulfur and aluminum The majority of the chemical plants are right smack in the heart of the black community. Black folks are tough they can take it I guess Some of the odors given off by the plants could make even the strongest of stomachs turn over.

Coming over the over-pass one can clearly see how polluted the air really is. Southern is a very unimposing physical plant. Most of the buildings are very old and scattered all over the place. The tennis courts are the first thing you see upon entering the campus and they are in complete disrepair. Blacks aren't really into tennis with the exception of Arthur Ashe of course

After one year of school I'm familiar with each and every building so the names are flashing through my mind as we ride through the campus. What a sight to see! All the black and beautiful faces. The greatest single collection of young black people anywhere since this is supposedly the largest black university in the world. The land of milk and honey for the male student with five females for each male.

Everything seemed typical during registration. It's the usual total confusion trying to get registered. Southern has the most archaic and inefficient system going I'm sure. Everything is spread out in fifty different directions so it's a big hassle trying to get your classes. The real problem comes though when you try to get your money since 98% of the students get some kind of financial aide

I'm on academic scholarship so I'm standing in line just like everybody else. Finally I get my money and head for the cashier's station. There aren't any more rooms available. This is a record breaking year I'm told. Over eight thousand students including thirty-two hundred freshmen. I'm impressed but I still don't have a place to stay.

On my way out of the gym who should appear but my brother Leon who just happens to be attending law school and is living in an apartment off-campus. How's it going Wayne? Leon asks. Fine except that I don't have anywhere to stay. What's wrong aren't there any rooms available he exclaims That's the story I heard. Well you can stay with me and then we can get the ghost out alright? The "ghost" being a 1965 galaxie 500. Sounds fine with me Leon.

With the case of my residency solved so smoothly I head triumphantly toward the student union.

It was inevitable that I run into Emily Semien and there she is standing in front of the union smiling as usual. Emily is from Opelousas and also of French descent so she has that funny sort of accent only a person from south Louisiana has. Her two front teeth are chipped. She's only about five feet tall but her body is very well proportioned. Her hips are very wide especially for one so small. I'm quite taken with her hips. Our relationship is somewhat strange, platonic as she likes to call it. She's forever flirting with me it seems. I like her very much and our relationship is very solid. She's quite intelligent and plans on becoming a lawyer Also she was a member of the 71 honors class which is how we met in the first place

Everyone thinks that we are going steady especially Mrs. Cobb who was our English instructor last year and also the sponsor of the freshman honors class

Upon sighting me Semien, which is my pet name for her begins to scream out my name as if I'm her long lost love who's just returned or something. Hey Semien what's happening? Finally managing to speak. We embrace and she kisses me on the cheek, which is very characteristic of her behavior toward me. Where are you staying Wayne? She inquires Oh I'm staying over on Fairchild with my brother I answer dutifully. Where are you staying Emily? I'm staying in Thomas Hall she answers. We sit and talk for what seems like over an hour about last year and all the good times we had dwelling mostly on the "Super Stupids" which is the name we gave ourselves. Everybody thought that was pretty cute since we were suppose to be the smartest freshman. We say our adieus and go our separate ways for the moment certain that we will see each other again real soon. Tomorrow probably.

The first day of class finally arrives and I find myself staring absent-mindedly at my schedule which says my first class is English 201. I guess you could say I'm suppose to start there, English 201 that is.

I had been going to this freshman biology seminar class for about three weeks now, a real boring class. A foreigner named Dr. Kakar was the instructor. A real nice guy but kind of hard to understand with his accent and all. The noise level in that class was unbelievable. There were about eighty students in class and there were about forty-one different conversations going on at the same time, not including the lecture.

So this one particular time I happen to come on late from my lab class and the only seat available is up front behind two young ladies. I slowly make my way to the seat, I'm immediately offered some cheetos by this extra slim coed. I accept a few not wanting to be anti-social even though I'm ??? to eat in class. She begins to giggle for some reason unknown to me. What's your name? she asks. I'm Wayne What's yours? Brenda" she says. Please to meet you Brenda. Same here Wayne. Who's your friend Brenda? Oh that's Linda she's a whiz at math she says nonchalantly. "Really" is the only thing I can think of at the moment to show that I'm impressed. What's the lecture about? trying to be studious. "Who cares" Brenda says, we all laugh. Brenda is about five feet five and weighs only ninety pounds with a perfectly shaped body. She could easily be a high fashion model, I silently think to myself. Her face is smooth and chestnut brown with an effervescent smile. She wears an afro

We talk the entire hour about music and blue jeans mostly. She likes every song that I like and she's very much into blue jeans evidenced by the fact she's presently wearing a pair of hip-hugger jeans which make her look very sexy indeed. She reminds me of a baby doll.

The lecture finally ends but not our new found romance because she agreed to go to McDonald's with me when I get my car. Now that I think about it I remember seeing Brenda once before with another guy walking hand in hand. She looked intriguing then for some unknown reason. Later I was to find out that that was her boyfriend named Toney, a very ordinary looking guy, homely in fact. A week later Leon and I go home to get my brother's 69 cougar which has a 390 engine in it and burns gas like a race car. On our way back to Baton Rouge the accelerator gets stuck and I almost have a wreck.

In class I tell Brenda I got the car and we are going to McDonald's after class. She says O.K.

Brenda decides she likes the car so it's ok for Linda to come with us. We make our way to the sign of the golden arches. I treat them to burgers, fries, and cokes. I'm enjoying my good fortune to the utmost and it seems as if they are doing the same.

Everything goes beautifully.

We take Linda home and Brenda has a five o'clock class so we drive back toward campus. Enroute we are holding hands and making eyes at each other. Is this Love? I ask Brenda. We both agree that this couldn't be anything else. The seed is planted.

I meet Brenda after her class and drive her over to her dorm, North Hall. Toney is waiting in the lobby when we enter so we act as if nothing has happened between us. A love triangle for sure because Toney is infatuated with Brenda anyone could tell that by the look on his face which fell somewhere between idolatry and hero-worship.

Where do I begin to tell the story of a young lady that came into my life and captured my imagination only to leave before I really got to know her. She was absolutely elegant. So perfectly thin and shapely that one could only describe her as being doll-like. Good vibes just naturally emanated from her. She was very beautiful on the inside. Her heart I'm sure was made of gold. She possessed an abundance of energy and a zest for life like no one I've ever met since.

She was forever wearing hip-hugger blue jeans, funny looking hats, 1920 style frock jackets that she got from her grandmother but never a dress, except for one time and that was a cause celebre for us.

Well anyway let me start from the beginning. I first met Brenda in a Biology 101 lab class, the instructor was from India or Pakistan or somewhere. His name was Dr. Kakar and he talked funny if you know what I mean. One day I was late for class and the only seat I could find was behind these two young ladies in the front row. One of them was Brenda and the other was her best friend named Linda. After sitting down and trying to look like a student I became aware of how thin and shapely Brenda's body was. I immediately began to stare at her. She was eating some cheeto's. I got up enough nerve to ask her what the seminar was about and she replied that she didn't know but that I could have some cheeto's. I took some and that was the beginning of our love affair. From that moment on to the end of the seminar we conversed non-stop. Everything that I liked she liked also, it was sort of unbelievable. Linda said that we should start going together since we had so much in common

The Accident

It was a Saturday night. I was driving the 1968 Cougar my brother Ernie has sold to me. It was white with beige interior. It had a 390 horsepower engine. Gorgeous car. Brenda and I were going to a party a friend of hers was having. Along for the ride were Brenda's best friend Mary and her boyfriend Sly. Everything seemed perfect and absolutely surreal. I was dating Brenda (love at first sight). I was sophomore in college with a fast beautiful car. What else could one ask for.

Everyone was excited. Laughter filled the air.

The 69 cougar had one fatal flaw..(maybe two), the car was a gas guzzler. The one and true fatal flaw was sometimes the accelerator would get stuck. The car would just take off like a rocket.

As we were approaching the red-light at the corner of scenic HWY and plank rd. I needed to get in the far left lane in order to make left turn. When I stepped on the gas pedal (as fate would have it) the accelerator got stuck. The cougar took off like a rocket. There was no wat I would be able to stop it before running into the cars that were waiting on the light to change. I switch off the ignition. The car had power steering. No way to control the car after that. I slammed on the brakes. The car crashed into the back of one of the cars waiting at the intersection. It had to be going at least 60 mph. fortunately no one was seriously injured. Brenda did not have even a scratch on her. My head and legs were bruised but most of all my ego. I considered myself an excellent driver before now. Mary was shaken but uninjured. Sly suffered the most. He had a cut above his left eye. We were all in a state of shock as we stood around observing the carnage. Headlights, bumpers, and various parts of the cougar and other cars were strewn all over the intersection. The people in the car that I had smashed into were swearing understandably.

In an instant my perfect world had come crumbling down. Sirens were screaming as the ambulance and police began to arrive. The paramedics put a bandage over Sly's eye and took him and Mary to the nearest hospital for observation. Brenda called her mom to come pick her up.

As I was giving my version of what had happened to the police officer I realized that the proof of insurance was back at the apartment that my brother Leon and I were renting,

I called Leon and informing him of what happened and that he needed to bring the insurance car down to the scene of the accident. Of course he said he would.

While waiting for Leon to arrive I had to make the most dreaded phone call of my life to Ernie to let him know that I had totaled one of the most beautiful cars that ever existed. Ernie was very sympathetic and understanding considering the circumstances. He said that the car was insured and surely we would get another one. Of course we never did.

In the meantime Leon finally arrives with the insurance card. For the previous 5 years (1968-1972) Leon had been attending the University of California at Berkeley. That being said, Leon and the police was not a good combination. Leon gets into an argument with one of the police officers. They end up handcuffing him and throwing him into the backseat of the police cruiser. They take us both to the nearest police precinct. Leon gets booked into jail on obstructing a police officer. Of course I get a ticket for failing to maintain control a vehicle among other things,

Leon ends up suspending the night in the slammer. Presently he's attending Southern University Law School so that morning his law school classmates go down and bond him out.

I ended up walking the 10 miles back to the apartment in the middle of the night. In total contrast to the way the night had begun.

The Elton John Concert

Can you believe we are going to the Elton John concert? I ask Brenda. She laughs that unmistakable laugh of hers and says yes…but we will probably be the only 2 black people there. True. The one thing that Brenda and I share is the love for the same songs.

We both love "Your Song" by Elton John which is the main reason behind us wanting to see him live in concert. We also love "Rocky Mountain High" by John Denver which is weird because he's a folk singer. I guess we both have eclectic taste.

Anyway the night of the concert arrives and I have to take the bus meaning public transportation since I wrecked the beautiful 1935 Mercury Cougar. As I'm walking down the street towards the coliseum a car pulls up beside me and its Brenda and her brother Bernie. Hey Wayne, Brenda yells while laughing, get in. we make our way to the coliseum. It's a sellout. Look at all the people I remark to Brenda. Finally we find our seats.

Full of excitement and anticipation we can't wait to hear Elton sing "Your Song" ....such a beautiful song. The crowd gives him standing ovation as he is being introduced. He sits down at his baby grand piano and begins to play. The crowd goes wild. Brenda and I are screaming and yelling. We are jumping up and down and hugging each other. It's as if we are in a dream. Still not believing we're seeing Elton John live and in concert. Very surreal out of the body experience.

He gives an amazing performance. We love all of the songs. Elton is a fantastic entertainer.

Trouble at School

Protests have been going on the entire fall semester. Students boycotting classes demanding the removal of the president Dr. Netterville. This particular morning students are gathering in front of the Administration Building demanding to meet with the Vice President of the Academic Affairs. Brenda and I are among the crowd of maybe 200 students. Brenda has on her bell bottom jeans and frock top that she swore she got from her grandmother. She looks as beautiful and elegant as a high fashion model. I am head over heels in love with her. All of a sudden out of nowhere we hear the sound of helicopters. They land and there are maybe 50 to 100 armed Louisiana State Troopers that emerge. They began firing teargas canisters into the crowed. Brenda and I began to run away from the scene. Widespread panic ensued. In the aftermath we found that 2 student had actually been mortally wounded by gunfire. Little did we know that our lives had been in jeopardy during those few fateful moments. The Governor ordered the campus closed and declared a state of emergency for Baton Rouge.

End of the Innocence

I returned home to northwest LA. Brenda was from Baton Rouge. How could something so wonderful and magical just end so suddenly. A puff of smoke disappearing into the wind. I was never to see Brenda again. When school resumed in the spring she transferred to Duke University. Fate can be terribly cruel at times.

One thing I know for sure is my heart was truly broken. Life for me was never the same after that. There is no greater feeling than being in love with someone.

The Criminal

Hey Mother, if anybody comes by or calls tell them I went to play tennis at the college. Sure Wayne I'll tell them, she replies. Thank you Mer.

Every time I get under the wheel of car I ??? fantasy about how I would look if this ???

It's a beautiful day. The sun is beginning to set on a clear humid southern evening. The tennis courts are empty. It seems as if I'm just out for the ride. While driving through the neighborhood next to mine whom should I run into but Ray. My best friend and also frequent joy-riding companion.

What's happening "Wayne Player" he says, calling me by my smoking name. You're what's happening is all I can think of at the moment.

Do you want to go to Houston with me to score this pound? he inquires. No, I don't think so, look how I'm dressed. That's O.K., he says you can go change and I'll come by to get you later. Alright, agreeing only half-heartedly. I drove all the way to Houston which is about 450 miles from home Kilo Louisiana.

Ray scores the pound of pot with no hassles and in no time we are on our way back home getting stoned out our minds. There ought to be a law against this high, don't you think Ray? There is Wayne, he says. Almost at that very instant blue flashing lights appear out of nowhere. It's the rollers Ray says calmly and matter-of-factly. I'm in total shock since there is a pound of marijuana under my feet. Ray pulls over to the side of the highway. Two typical back country Texas style red-neck cracker policemen are suddenly upon us pointing 38 caliber pistols in our faces. What's wrong? Ray asks. Let me see your driver's license boy", one of them says laughingly. Get out of the car is the next command given to Ray. While all of this is going on I'm frozen stiff with fear because I know there is no way they are going to miss this pot if they decide to search the car.

One officer begins to search the car, while the other interrogates Ray on the outside of the car. During all this time they still haven't told us why they stopped us in the first place. Suspicion I guess. Land of the free, home of the brave seems more like a police state at the moment to me anyway. Get out of the car nigger the officer commands me after finishing his search of the driver's side. I'm busted for sure I think to myself. I get out of the car and he immediately pushes me against the car and tells me to raise my hands and spread my legs while at the same time slapping me across the head with a black leather strap. He continues his search of the car and almost instantly finds the pot. He lets out a rebel yell and exclaims to his fellow policeman, "Look what I found" holding the dope up in the air. They handcuff us and take us to the Hemphill County Jail. Some more interrogations and beatings with the strap, racial slurs laughter. Finally they book us with possession of marijuana with intent to distribute. How in the hell they knew we planned on distributing it puzzled me. Can we make a phone call? Ray asks. The answer is no and the pigs lead us up the steps to the cells which are replete with gallow. This frightens me a little. Gallows in this day and age. I mean it's 1976. Jail for the first time. The cell is filthy with a commode right in the middle, a center-piece I surmise. It's hard for me to think of myself as criminal but that's exactly what I am at the moment. All sort of thoughts begin to run through my head. Suppose I get put in prison for 5 years over some weed this is absurd. I'm ruined. Just graduated from college this past fall, in Pre-Med no less, and here I am stuck in this nasty cell. What's my mom going to say I ask Ray, he shakes his head in the negative I'm so ashamed of myself.

Time takes on a new dimension in jail. An hour seems like an entire day. The morning finally comes. There are two or three people walking around downtown which looks like a set out of an old western with hitches for your horses. We both yell out of the window to try to get somebody's attention. One of them hears us and stops. It's an elderly black lady. We give her our names and phone numbers back home and she agrees to deliver our message. After 35 hours in jail our parents show- up. I felt like going through the floor when my Mom and Dad appeared at the cell door. They were so nice and loving I almost cried.

At he kangaroo court the judge charged us 1000 dollars plus the cost of court, which was 25 dollars.

I felt sorry for my Dad. We all could see it was just a racket for the police to collect money. There was no record of the case.

My Mother the Movie Star

I've always wondered why I loved old black and white gangster films, especially the ones with Humphrey Bogart and James Cagney in them. The one that comes to mind is the "Roaring Twenties". Well anyway bear with me for I diverge from the main story here.

One day while at my mom's house going through some old photos I came across a small wallet size photograph of my mother. It was very, very old and cracked. She must have taken it when she was in her late teens or early twenties. Bear in mind that she is now seventy-five years old, three-quarters of a century. It was sepia-toned. That must have been a popular form for photos during the thirties.

I decided to have this tattered and worn photograph restored if at all possible. The first so-called photographer I took it to charged me two-hundred dollars and the result looked as if it had been made from a copier. I was so disappointed but I paid the fraud anyway since it had taken six-weeks and I desperately wanted to send my mom a copy. Being totally unimpressed with my first attempt at having the picture restored I took it to Sears. Yes that Sears of Sears and Roebuck fame. I had to wait another six-weeks.

Absolutely drop-dead gorgeous! The photograph was sepia-toned like the original. I was astounded by the restoration. The clerk said they had taken a picture of the original and then an artist had painted in the part that was worn and tattered. Also it only cost me eighty-nine dollars this time. My mom had movie* star good-looks. That explains everything! My mother was a movie-star!! Oh! How I love old black and white movies!

I like old things. Antiques
old black and white films
especially with Bogart
Victorian furniture
old houses with high ceilings
impressionists paintings
Paris, France
springtime romance
slender women
with long waists
croquet
two-seater Mercedes
Alfa Romeos
Cameras bicycles
Tennis and chess

I guess you could say it was my lucky day when I found this typewriter for sale at the thrift shop for five dollars and fifty cents. It seems to be in perfect working order as for as I can tell. There doesn't seem to be a thing wrong with it. It's so old and antique that I just fell in love with it the first time that I saw it. And the price I could not believe! Sometimes it just pays to be at the right place at the right time. Well it seems as if there is going to be a baseball strike that is going to spoil a great season for a number of players especially Matt Williams of San Francisco. He already has 3 home runs and it's only the first week in August. He's on pace to break Babe Ruth's and Roger Maris's all-time records. Cest La Vie I guess but it really is a shame. I'm in love with life at the moment. Everything is lovely. I have a gorgeous old house with high ceilings great windows. An old Schwinn bicycle (red no less). Things could not be any better unless I hit the lotto for eight million dollars at this point anything is possible even the publishing of my manuscript for a screenplay about Brenda Jamin Washington. The love of my life when I was in college. Baseball as a metaphor for life. Three strikes and you're out. Two outs in the bottom of the ninth, no balls and two strikes on the batter. Down by one run in the seventh game of the world series. My favorite things, black and white movies (very old) jazz photography antiques beautiful women. I met a beautiful lady today. She wanted directions to twenty east. Of course I showed her the way she was driving a black Nissan Stanza she was red and freckled face and beautiful

The Instigator

I only want peace on earth and good will toward men yet I get labeled as an instigator. I don't understand it. Everybody's always telling me their story. What do they want from me? I try to be understanding of everyone's point of view maybe that's what wrong. I probably should tell them to get lost or go jump in a lake somewhere. But that's not the way I operate.

People are afraid of the truth. One would rather lie it seems than tell the truth about a situation. People are weird is the only way I can describe it. Complex but yet absolutely and positively strange can one not have an opinion or should I say can I have an opinion without everyone getting upset. We all are going to die any way. What's the problem? Afraid to die probably yes! Get a life dog! Put a little music in your life please. Keep my opinions to myself. Do my own life story.

This Old House

I'd always wanted an old house with high ceilings and hardwood floors for some reason I can't explain. They always seem to be so elegant in magazines such as modern architecture. I finally bought one and it has brought me even more joy than I anticipated. I marvel at the 13 foot ceilings and detailed windows. There is such a sense of roominess. It was constructed in 1935 according to my property deed. The first time I read that made me feel so proud. I love antiques. I'll never forget the reaction of Earvin whose my best friend and frequent chess and tennis partner the first time he came over to play chess. He said and I quote "Wayne, I love this house! You went and bought yourself a mansion". I smiled and said thanks of course but I wouldn't call it a mansion by no stretch of the imagination. I do know that it would be an impossibility for him to love it as much as I do. There are no hardwood floors but plenty of carpet in my favorite color taupe. Also rosewood. It has a fireplace. But more than that it has character. Maybe I've stumbled upon something here!

Pam

A lady
held in
high esteem
She could do
no wrong
at least
to me it seemed
then one day
cruel words
she spoke
piercing my heart
as a dagger
would cloak
stunned and hurt
I watched
???
fall into
the dirt

Before

Feeling
the pain
of love
again
Hurting inside
but knowing
I tried
to love
once more
as I did
before

POEM FOR MYESHA

The thought
of you
brings instant tears
to my eyes
the sight of you
can brighten up
even the darkest skies
with the sound
of your voice
All my troubles
cease
how proud I am
that you're
my niece

BROKEN DREAMS

Life is but
broken dreams
reflected in a
golden pond
it seems,
full of thought
and scores
of battles
yet to be fought

Run To

Nowhere to run,
Trapped by
the rays
of the
blinding sun,
Frozen
is my mind,
Lost in
the search
of trying
to find,
What lies
beyond the hill
on yonder's rise

Wayne
11/15/81

Hopeless

Without hope
I cling
to the ever
unraveling rope
of life
that slowly
comes apart
each day
at dawn
right before
my very eye
Even though
I live
I've still
begun to die

WHEN AT FIRST WE MET
(First Sighting)

The first time that I saw Brenda (she was a phantom of delight) she was walking across campus holding hands with another guy. They seemed to enjoy each other's company immensely. She was giggling and smiling. Laughing at something the guy with her was saying. Upon hearing her laugh it seemed as if I could feel that she was a very special lady. She had good vibrations. I loved the way she was dressed. She had on hip-hugger jeans with bell bottoms and shoes called clogs. She had a very long waist. Very slim and petite lady. Elegant I would say. Two ships passing in the night. Me walking alone on the sidewalk in front of the library. She walking with her boyfriend on grass in the sunshine in the middle of the day on a perfect fall day. Cool, crisp and sunny. Never thought that I would see her again. I kept on going my merry way but with the sound of her laughter forever etched in my mind.

I. The First Sighting
A. She was with a guy walking across the lawn
B. The laugh
C. The sound of her voice

(A Short Story)
A Broken Ankle (Fractured Fibula)

I've been playing tennis for over 30 years. I remember watching Arthur Ashe Win Wimbledon in 1975. The championships Wimbledon is such a classy and elegant tennis tournament that it is almost lyrical and poetic. As a matter of fact it's on this week and I've been watching all the matches, especially men's singles. I wish I could serve and volley! Sorry. Back to the story. On June 15, 1997 at about 9 p.m. I was attempting to take a forehand crosscourt return in a doubles match, when I severely twisted my ankle. I heard something crack (as a matter of fact two cracks) it happened in slow motion first the twist, then the two cracks and I crumpled to the court. A new experience! It did not hurt as bad as I had imagined breaking a bone would. Rutnard, my doubles partner came running over me and asked if I was O.K. Then immediately pronounced, laughingly I might add, "Ain't nothing wrong with you man, get up". To which I replied, "Yes there is, this is serious."

I find out at 3:30 p.m. that I've fractured my ankle in two places. Actually my fibula. Some emergency. They put a soft cast on it and give me some crutches and a prescription for pain-killers. They tell me I need to make an appointment with an orthopedic specialist. Two days later I get a permanent cast. It has to stay on 4-6 weeks. I'm thinking this must be a dream. I've never been injured seriously in my life. There's a first time for everything I guess. Two weeks have passed as I tell my tale of woe??? Thirty years is a lifetime. My father died in 89. What's a fractured fibula compared to that. Life is full of tragedies.

Sometimes

Sometimes,
in my mind
at least,
I can
still
hear
your laughter,
And then,
I begin
to wait
for the
smile
that comes
after

Wayne

The Story of Brenda

How does one capture the essence of a person, especially a woman that was so unique in her own way. She was so thin and elegant that I'm quite sure she could have a been a model. Very long-waisted with nice legs, even though she hardly ever wore a dress except this one time which is a story within itself. I say woman although at the time we met we were just teenage college freshmen. I can remember the first time I ever saw her. She was walking with a male companion on the opposite sidewalk in front of the library. As we were passing she laughed out loud, such an unusual and lovely laugh that I was startled. What a wonderful laugh I thought to myself as I looked at her across the street. She had on hip-hugger bell-bottomed blue jeans. What a sight to behold on such a thin and elegant and long-waisted woman

One week later I find myself rushing to my Biology 101 lab class because I'm late. As I enter the seminar room to a packed house it seems there is not an empty seat to be found. As I wander toward the front of the room lo and behold an empty seat appears. Hurriedly I sit down besides these two lovely co-eds

Regina

She's
a beauty
and a
sight
to behold
satin voice
and a
heart
of gold
these things
I know
for I've
been told

Wayne

Helaire/Davis
Public
Relations

Elegant
antiques
watches,
pens

There's
more to
life

More to life

Working
everyday
like
a machine
never, ever
managing
to
come clean
but
what does
it mean!
Is
there
more
to
life
than
it seem

More to Life.

Working
everyday
like
a machine,
never, ever
managing
to
come clean
but
what
'Does
it mean?
is there
move'
to life
than
it seems

Wayne
1/19/00

I am
my father
and my mothers
son
what
have
the two
of
then done
brought
me forth
and made
me one

"The Meaning of Life"

Where is my father? Daddy died on April 28, 1989. I was at home when Leon called me to try me that he had passed away. News as devastating as that just doesn't sink in at first. You hear it. You understand it. But still it just does not register in your brain. I guess it's called denial. But at that moment it was if I had ceased to exist myself. In a way, because I am half of my father and half of my mother genes, I did lose part of my genetic composition. Part of my father is in me. All of God is in all of mankind. The essence of life. How can something so beautiful and mysterious as the gift of life be bestowed on one. The ability to breathe, to see, to touch, to hear etc. And all the complexities that are involved in these processes where do all the creatures (man included) that inhabit the earth came from? The plants? Questions? Questions? Where is my father? Knowing one day that I shall suffer the same fate I ask God what does it mean to live and die like countless others before me?

Monday Night
Atlanta

Dear Mother,

How are you doing? I'm doing fine myself just working too much I think. Are you going to Myesha's graduation (I'm sure you are, just checking) I'm going to try to make it but I'm not sure because I want to come home for Christmas but will let you know. Tell Aunt Emma Lee and Verogers I said hello. It felt so good talking to Elsie. I just really hate that I didn't get to see her.

How's Uncle Poker? Tell him that I said hello and that he is in my prayers. How have you and Leon been getting along lately? I'm sure he still worries you to death. Tell Rhonda hello and that I'm praying everyday that everything goes well with her pregnancy.

I still haven't gotten my film developed with some pictures of the house on it but hopefully I will this week. Will send you some as soon as I get them. I really miss you and only wish that I could visit more often but you're always on my mind.

Two Women

There are these two women at work that don't like each other at all. They are both black females. That's about the only thing that they have in common. One of them is the most stylish and elegant woman a man would ever want to meet. Very attractive. Maybe that explains it. She's sweet, kind, gracious, statuesque, intelligent and athletic. She inspires love and admiration in men. The other woman is very cold, moody, rude almost sadistic in nature. She seems to enjoy pain. Inflicting mental pain on people to the point where one just wants to maim her. They've come to blows twice. The two had an epic verbal and physical confrontation a few weeks back which by the way is the basis or I should say inspiration for this story. A so-called psychiatrist was called in to talk to them.

Dear Mother,

It was great seeing you for the few days we spent together last month. I enjoyed every minute of it. Thanks for the biscuits and gumbo. They were fantastic as usual. I was so happy to finally make to one of Gerald's houses. They have a beautiful place.

Now is the time for all good men to come to the aid of the their country for once in my life.

For once in my life photo exhibit Moneta Sleet famous photograpyher from Ebony and Jet is in town for the Black Arts festival. Avery Brooks from Spenser is the artistic director for the whole affair in ??? I probably should volunteer for something but do not feel up to it been kind of down lately for some unknown reason could it be I'm just getting older and just plain tired of the grind of every day life. The constant droning of people unhappy people complaining about every thing you could imagine life has finally beaten me down it seems finally got the best of me knock me to the floor with a left hook to the chin square flush end of round saved by the bell live to tight the final round to fight the final round fight the final final final round final round final round round final round final round

The Fall of 1981

Her name was Carol Annett Wright. I should have gotten married to her. She was such a sweet and loving woman with long sexy legs. The first time we met we had a little argument or I should say a slight disagreement over something minor at work. I was certain that she hated me since I almost never had an argument with a lady, especially at work. But, to my total surprise one day she walked up to me and said, "Hi, my name is Carol." Then she reached around me and out her hand in my back pocket and said, call me. That was so sexy I thought to myself. I smiled and said you bet I'll call you. She laughed and walked away. Little did I know at them time that this would be the beginning of a beautiful relationship, to paraphrase Bogart. I called Carol that night and we talked for 3 hours. From that day forward for almost 6 months we were each other constantly. Day and night. We worked together from 12 midnight to 8am. We were together from the time we got off to work until it was time to, get ready to go, back to work, we were inseparable and I loved and enjoyed every second of our relationship. To quote a line form one of my favorite songs, "We had it all, just like Bogie and Bacall, starring in our own late, late show, ailing away to Key Largo". We shopped. We laughed. We went to dinner and a movie. We washed and folded clothes together. Sometimes Carol would cook dinner for us. I truly loved Carol and I'm sure she loved me.

We had out pet names for each other. She called me Wayne-Wayne and I called her Care-Care. Where that came from I will never know. Why we never got married can't be explained. How we ever broke up remains a mystery. The constant being together at work and at home somehow got the best of us. However, those six months together were idyllic.

"Tis better to have loved and lost, than never to have loved at all."

Broken Bone

I've been
knocked low
bruised
and
battered
from head
to toe
shattered
bones

I've been
knocked
on so low
bruised
and
battered
from
head to
toe
shattered
bones
was
the blow
done
in vain
just
for show

Wayne Films Ltd
Old Black and White Photographs Restored

Black and White Photography
Antique Watches
Tennis
Wimbledon
French Open
Chess
Morphy
Western Forest
Duncanson
Impressionist
Van Gogh
The Starry Night
Casablanca
As Time Goes By
BMW
Alfa Romeo
MGA 1959
Red or Black Ferrari

KAMELDA

She sits
there
Quietly
In
All her
Charm,
Never a
soul
Would she
harm,
She stole
My heart
And kept
It warm

Wayne

When At First We Met

It was
bright and sunny
that fateful day
when I just
happened to see
your face
love at first sight
I think they say
my heart
was smitten
with love
that day
when at first
we met that way
(for Melba)

"Puppy Love"

Why is Melba sad? I do not know because she says that she can not tell me at the moment. She will tell me later whenever that is. I can not imagine what the problem is. She does know that she is sad however. I asked her to marry me which is really unbelievable to me and she said that she had to think about it for a while. I asked her to go to Paris with me and she was undecided! Paris in the springtime is my idea of romantic but maybe she does not feel the same, but she did love Casablanca and that made me happy. I remember the first time we met, it was at the swimming pool one summer day. I thought that she was the cutest girl in the world. She was very pretty indeed. I just had to talk to her, this little dark doe-eyed beauty. I don't recall how I got up the courage to go and ask her what her name was but I did end up following her home on my little purple bike with the white banana seat. She gave me her phone number. We talked a lot that summer. I would call her and play this song called "Make Me Yours" by Betty Swann. I loved that song and I loved Melba. "Puppy Love" I think they call it.

Wayne
1/15/96

Beauty

What does
it
means
to be
beautiful?
No one
knows
but yet
when one
sees
a beautiful
sunset,
a bright
orange
moon
as full as
it can get,
one often
remarks
what a
lovely sunset
or
what a
gorgeous
moon
as elusive
as a fresh
spring breeze

"Beauty
will save
the world"

Time and Motion

Thoughts
pass
briefly
through
my mind
leaving
traces
of
days
gone by
tears
roll
down
my
swollen
face

Thoughts
pass briefly
through my
mind,
tears
roll down
my
swollen face

"The Sky At Night"

I see you
in the sky
at night
among the stars
shining bright
I love it
most
when
you're within
my sight

The way is clear
loving you
is so easy
my dear
with you
beside me
the way
is clear

Before

Before we
had such
loneliness

Together
we've
found true
happiness
what
more
can two people
ask
for
I guess...

Wayne

Carrie Helaire

Dark and sweet
as a
chocolate bar
beautiful
and bright
as a
far away
star
soft and cool
as a
summer breeze
all these
things
she is
to me
Carrie Helaire
is
my mother
you see

G. Davis
8/24/97

The
Sky
At Night

"The Sky At Night"

When you
smile at me

Whenever
you are
within
my sight

I see
you
in the
sky
at night
among the
stars
shining bright
I love it
when
you're within
my sight

I love
you
more
each
and
every
day

Old
adventures in advertising
new
adventures in advertising
Major motion picture being filmed at Trammel Crowe Park...8/22/29

Excalibur has sunk beneath the waves......Godspeed Glenn

A Heavenly Place

Mother,
whenever I think
of you
A smile
comes to
my face,
knowing that
you are
resting
in
a
heavenly
place

Before

Before,
we had
such loneliness,
together
we've found
true happiness,
what more
can two people
ask for
I guess.

Wayne

What in the World.

(Am I Doing Here)

I sit and
think
what in the world
am I doing here
At this moment
in time
which is instantly
gone,
leaving me
alone
with my thoughts
on my
so-called
life
here in
paradise,
dogwoods
in bloom
beautiful music
playing
softly in
my room

My (Wayne's) Favorite Things

Antique furniture
Black & white
photography
Old movies
black & white
Antique watches,
vintage sport
cars
MGA's 1955
Tennis
Chess
Impressionist
Paintings
Van Gogh
Wimbledon
French Open

Adventures
in
Advertising...
Musings..

Today my life stood still
once she appeared before
my very eyes as if some divine
lovely incarnation of beauty,
a sight to behold a thing of beauty
is a joy and delight the most wonderfully
gorgeous woman I've ever met a beauty beyond
compare standing right in front of me with a
smile so sweet and lovely she spoke with
a smooth silky voice
without a choice
I fell completely
head over heels in love at first sight

I fell in love at first sight today
I met the most gorgeous and lovely
woman that I have ever had the good
fortune to meet as if I could dream up
an absolutely drop dead gorgeous movie star

Nothing Can Hurt Me Now

What a cruel blow
The most kind
And sweetest person
I know
I can't talk
To anymore
Nothing can
hurt me
now
No way
No how,
My hurt is
too deep,
All those memories
I've got to keep,

Ann Horne

She comes
to me
In my
lonely dreams
Only to
disappear
In along with
the morning
it seems
she
and the
moon
were
there last
night,
now
they're
both
out
of sight

???
there
quietly
in
all her
charm,
never a
soul
would she
harm,
she stole
my heart
and kept
it
warm.

Broken Hearted

Standing
alone
in the
morning
rain,
wondering
whether
I should
ever
love
someone
again.

Broken hearted
standing
alone
in the
morning
rain,
wondering
whether
I should
ever love
someone
again

You sit there
quietly in
all your charm
with style
and grace
surrounding
your
lovely face

She
sits there
quietly
in all her charm

Quietly
in all
your charm
never a
soul
would you harm

You sit
there
quietly
with
your
lovely face
style and grace
surrounded
by

Kamelda
you sit
there
quietly
with
your
lovely face
surrounded
by
style and grace

In all
her charm
never a
soul
would
she
harm
take
my
heart
and
keep it warm

With
the
sound
of your
voice
I have
no
choice
but to
surrender
my heart

Just to
touch
your hand
would be
so grand
to see
you
laugh
and
then smile

I hang
to
hold you
for a
little while,
just to
see you laugh
and then
to see your

smile
just to
touch
your hand
would be
so grand

I long
to hold
you
for a
little
while,
just to
hear
you laugh
and then to
see you
smile
to touch
your
hand
would
be so
grand

I surrendered
my heart
from the
very start
I gave
you
my all
both
big and
small

AWAY

Away from you
another day
not knowing
what to say
only thinking
of past times
that were so sweet
and waiting till
the next time
we meet

WHO'S LUCY

Lucy is the water
that makes up
the ocean
of my mind
She's the countless waves
that splash
upon the shores
of my brain
from loving her
I can't refrain
my love for her
shall always remain
despite the pain
I might incur
by giving
all my love to her

Wayne Films Ltd
Old black and white photographs restored

Black and White Photography
Antique Watches
Tennis
Wimbledon
French Open
Chess
Morphy
Western Forest
Duncanson
Impressionist
Van Gogh
The Starry Night
Casablanca
As Time Goes By
BMW
Alfa Romeo
MGA 1959
Red or Black Ferrari

The meaning of life as I see it. It a complete mystery in my eyes. Which came first? The chicken or the egg? Where did man come from? Was he created by God? Where did God come from? I do know that I exist at this moment. The world is full of people in different parts of the earth there's the sun moon and stars. Plants and animals. The weather changes from hot to cold and vice versa. I get old. I was born on 9/30/53. It's now 11/23/94. Time passes. My father died 4/28/89. Life is beautiful. So many things to see. A gorgeous sunrise a fantastic sun set. A full moon sky full of stars twinkling in the far off horizon. What lies beyond is unknown. One second passes and I am infinitely changed by it's passing??? do I pretend as if I don't know how to write when in reality that's what I'm supposed to be a very humorous witty charismatic charming human being. Women find me interesting for some unknown reason at least it's unknown to me. They say you're interesting and laugh or smile

(To Melba)

I long
to hold
you,
for a
little while,
just to
hear
you laugh
and then
to see
you smile,
and then,
for a moment
to hear
you speak,
these small
treasures
are all
I seek

Wayne
11/26/98

Dear K

I miss you dearly, especially your warm and engaging smile. We made such sweet music together! "We had it all, just like Bogie & Bacall, starring in our own late, late show, sailing away to Key Largo." I can hardly wait for our next photo/tennis session.

P.S.
1. P-K4 ....

The Job

How can they call this work when the people here are on the verge of a nervous breakdown it seems. We have the neurotic bosses that think they are some sort of God or should I say demi-gods! They want you to do five things at once. Do they not realize that in a laboratory situation one needs ample time to complete one's analysis and to repeat said analysis if results are not satisfactory. You do need some margin for error. Why they do not understand is a mystery to me. Will someone please inform me as to why. There is an adversarial relationship between supervisors and the technicians that are suppose to perform the everyday routine analyses. They want you to do all the tests without ever making a mistake. Input data into the computer, make all necessary reagents, wash all the glassware, clean-up the area etc. These things do tend to wear on the nerves ever so slightly to the point where you feel fatigued but don't know the reason why especially mentally exhausted.

How did it all fall apart? That's a very good question! Let us begin by saying I never said & ??? she was such a sweet lady. When she came into my life seven years ago. I must say I never thought it would work. She was my childhood sweetheart that had gotten married right after high school and I went off to college.

???lasback:

And so the story begins. It's a warm summer day. I'm riding my purple bike with a white banana shaped seat. I'm feeling great on top of the world it seems. I ride merrily along by the swimming pool. Lo and behold! The cutest little girl that I've ever laid eyes on. Love at first sight. Somehow I had to meet her. She was a phantom of delight. As if in a dream I nervously make my way toward her you're the prettiest girl I've ever seen! What's your name I ask. She giggles and says Melba. I fall hopelessly in love at that moment. I can't help but smile. I end up walking her home. At least I rode my bike along side her. So this is love. A most unforgettable walk. I end up talking to her on the phone almost everyday that summer. The hit song was "Make Me Yours" by Bettye Swan. I'll never forget Melba or that song.

Thanksgiving
1998

I've never been one to get hyped up about Thanksgiving especi??? since the ones I remember most are the one's of my adolescence at my mom & dad's house my mother is a gourmet cook so the food was always delectable and plentiful. They were always joyous and wonderful occasions. Everybody was always happy and thankful to be alive. Could my memories possibly be as beautiful and pleasant as I recall. I'm sure there must have been some kind of acrimony or rancor somewhere in our midst but it never surfaced during our Thanksgiving dinner. The only topics of discussion were football and how great the food was.

Fast forward to 1998 there's no aroma of any kind in my house. Only the sound of music. I've split up with my fiancé although we still talk. She has invited me over to her apartment for dinner. Her mother and brother (youngest) have driven up from Louisiana. As a matter of fact I had to rescue them from the darkened streets of Atlanta last night because of the directions or I should say lack of directions given them by my sweetheart Baby Doll (my pet name for my fiancé these days') is not very good at giving out directions I love her laugh and smile and petulant behavior whenever I kid her on any subject.

You're
standing
next
to me
I feel
so
proud
as if
my
head
were
in the
clouds

Like
the sky
at
night

The
sky
at
night

When
you smile
it's like
the
sky at
night
full of
stars

and shining
bright

To
me
you're
like
the sky
at
night
with the
moon
and stars
shining
bright

I love to
have you
in
my sight
as if
you were
the sky
at night
full of stars
and shining bright

My Favorite Things

Mom,
Antique watches and furn
Old coins
Black and white
Old movies
Photography
Sepia
Schwinn
Impressionism
Chess
Music
Poetry
Two-seater
Mercedes
Tennis

Helaire/Wayne Public Relations
2/3/6

Glory days
Golden days
Golden

Chessmaster 4000

Title Human vs Expert 9-2-2000
White Human
Black: Expert
Date: 9-2-2000

1.	d2-d4	d7-d5
2.	e2-e3	g8-f6
3.	f1-d3	e7-e6
4.	f2-f4	f8-d6
5.	g1-f3	c7-c5
6.	c2-c3	b8-c6
7.	f3-e5	c8-d7
8.	0-0	c5-c4
9.	02	0-0
10.	d2	a8-c8
11.	f3	d8-c7
12.	c1-d2	c7-b6
13.	b2-b3	c4xb3
14.	a2xb3	a7-a5
15.	g2-g4	f8-d8
16.	g4-g5	f6-e4
17.	d2-e1	c6xe5
18.	f3xe5	d6xe5
19.	f4xe5	e4xg5
20.	e1-h4	h7-h6
21.	h4xg5	h6xg5
22.	d1-h5	g7-g6
23.	h5xg5	d7-b5
24.	f1-f4	b6-c7
25.	c3-c4	d5xc4

26.	a1-f1	f7-f5
27.	e5xf6ep	c4xb3
28.	g5xg6+	g8-f8
29.	f4-h4	c7-h7
30.	h4xh7	b7-b6
31.	h7-h8++	..

;Game over: Black is checkmated.

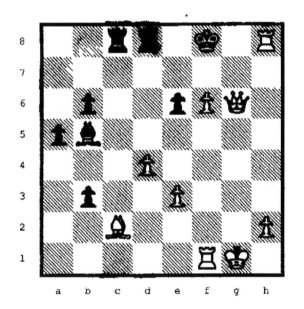

90

SECONDTHOUGHTS

A collection of poems by Wayne

SECOND THOUGHTS

Once I thought
I wanted love
as sure as
I wanted
the heavens above
but now I've got
second thoughts
about seeking
love like I
once sought
for no matter
how honest
one is
it can still
bring tears
and cries
of love
that no one hears

SOMETIMES

Sometimes,
in my mind,
I can still
hear your laughter
and then
I begin
to wait
for the
smile that
comes after

EMPTY

My life's
been empty
from the moment
you left
if only I had
held you tighter
and told you
how I really felt
then kissed
your lips
a thousand times
while I had
the chance
to find
for sure
true romance

PERHAPS

Watching the world
and it's
endless sights
while lonesome days
turn into nights
thinking thoughts
of if I ever might
get a chance
to see
Perhaps
what love
is really like

SEMIEN CAME

People come
and people go
where to
I'll never know
into tunnels
or out in the snow

The sharing
of joy
passes by
and in its wake
sorrows lie

LUCKY LUCKY ME

You may ask
how lucky
can a man be?
Some might say
as lucky
as the sun and sea
both of which
are free from worry
unlike you and I
but I've met you
you see
Lucky lucky me

YOU'RE

YOU'RE the
fresh morning dew
that falls
at dawn
you're the only one
to which
my heart'll respond
you're sweet honey
from the honeybee's hive
you're a beautiful lake
in which
I'd like to dive

BROKENHEARTED

By mere chance
we were fortunate
enough to meet
and never have I known
a love so sweet
every word she ever
spoke to me
were like rays of sunshine
flush upon my face
warming me inside
and if my ears
could taste
her voice would be
like honey
thrust upon my tongue
leaving me to wonder
what's my life become
since we met
and parted
locking me
in the cage
of the brokenhearted

THOUGHTS

Thoughts
of you
keep me
from falling
into the depths
of despair
for other
than you
I haven't
a care

ALMOST- for Brenda

Once upon a time
I could see
the twinkle in your eye
But now
we both live
under different parts
of the sky
Although
I think of you
often
thoughts never soften
this longing
I have for you
Almost
but they never do

UNCERTAINTY

Why live today
or even tomorrow
drowning in your
own sorrow
not knowing
what's real
or what's for real
not knowing what to feel
or even how to feel
when the one
you love
has gone away
to stay
leaving you
alone
to sing
the song
only the brokenhearted know
Uncertainty in
your mind
uncertainty is unkind

ALL'S THAT'S LEFT

THE Moments
I spent
with you
were just
a joyous few
touched
with the splendor
of the setting sun
blessed
with the freshness
of a new day
that's come
Now that
you're gone
and I'm
all alone
All that's left
is the joy
I felt
upon learning
your name
while holding
your hand
in the
morning rain

FAITH

Hoping
when there's
no hope left
feeling
when there's
nothing
to be felt
living
even though
life's a burden
loving
although
heartbreak is certain

FIRST TIME

Meeting you
for the first time
was like hearing
a wind chime
sing a song
of love
played upon it
by the
unseen wind
but then
it was yet unknown
that love
would come
between us

RAINBOW

Rainbow rainbow
so pleasing
to thine eye
Oh how, oh how
such beauty
in yonder sky
appears before
one's very eyes
once rain
has come and said
goodbye

REALITY

You've sunken
deep into my life
even deeper
than my marrow
you make me feel
like a spring morning
filled with the song
of an ascending sparrow

STILL

Can't sit still
it's against
my will
must move round
got to hear
some sound
look what I found
movement slowed down
on a picture
no less
I must confess
I'm most impressed
with stillness
I guess

MARY MAUDE

You took my heart
by storm
with your smile
so soft and warm
And I
taken totally
by surprise
can now
suddenly realize
the woman
you really are
shining brightly
as if
some far away star

Alone

The sounds of silence
knock upon my walls
while the thought
of loneliness calls
for me to come
to her den
And then
I realize
That I'm alone
For time and time
again
it has been shown
that love has
spread its wings
and flown
once one
has to be alone

AMERICA

Where dreams
come true
and
nightmares too
parole denied
while
the president lied
suspicions confirmed
about lessons
unlearned
from her
glorious past
Can America last?

JUSTIFIED LADY

What are women for?
to love, cherish
and adore?
to have and to hold
to shelter
one from the cold
for the times
when life's loneliness
sets in cause then
only a woman
can bring the joy
back again
And when a man
finds a lady
to share his hopes
only then
can he cope

"Beauty Will Save The World"

The Autobiography of Wayne Helaire

What does
it mean
to be alive?
Father died
then
mother passed,
I can't
take it
anymore
wondering
what other
tragedies,
life
has in store

St Maarteen,

It's beautiful down here. What a lovely quaint and old-fashioned island it seems to be. We are right on the Caribbean Sea with ships sailing by our patio. Yachts, sailboats .. A gorgeous sight, very picturesque.

Rented a car and drove around the island. It's divided into a Dutch side and a French side St Martin (St Maarteen). There are so many bars and restaurants and shops etc. We are going to take a day trip to the Island of Anguilla which is suppose to have the most beautiful beaches.

Went downtown to the Royal Islander Club visited a couple of shops. Bought a couple of ships in a bottle as a gift for some people back home. Got some beautiful post cards to send. Had big fun at the Casino Royale. Had dinner at the Paris Bistro (French Restaurant)

Printed in the United States
By Bookmasters